The Whispering Woods

Mrigendra Bharti

Published by Sellbrochure Vymish Entertainment, 2024.

This is a work of fiction. Similarities to real people, places, or events are entirely coincidental.

THE WHISPERING WOODS

First edition. June 28, 2024.

ISBN: 979-8227149886

Written by Mrigendra Bharti.

Table of Contents

Preface

Dear Reader,

Welcome to the world of "The Whispering Woods," a place where imagination reigns supreme and talking animals share their secrets with curious children. This book isn't just a collection of stories; it's a journey back to the boundless creativity of childhood, where fantastical creatures whispered secrets in the rustling leaves and brave princesses defied expectations.

The stories within these pages were born from a simple desire – to revisit the joy of storytelling I experienced as a child. Scribbling tales in dusty notebooks under the shade of a banyan tree, I filled them with talking animals, mischievous fairies, and princesses yearning for adventure. These were stories that fueled my imagination and nurtured my dream of becoming a writer.

Years passed, and my life took me down different paths. I became known for writing novels that tackled complex social issues, stories far removed from the whimsical world of talking animals. Yet, a part of me yearned to revisit that childhood haven, the place where stories bloomed effortlessly from the fertile ground of imagination.

One day, I unearthed a dusty box filled with those old notebooks. As I reread the faded ink, a sense of nostalgia washed over me, reminding me of the unadulterated joy of storytelling. I realized that the essence of these stories remained timeless – the simple joy of weaving fantastical tales, the unfiltered expressions of emotions, and the boundless belief in the power of imagination.

And so, "The Whispering Woods" came to life. With each tale, I relived the thrill of creating worlds unseen, breathing life into characters who spoke through the rustling leaves and trickling streams. The stories are far from perfect; they are a testament to the raw, unbridled creativity of childhood, untouched by the complexities of adult life.

But within these imperfections lies a magic that transcends age. These stories are meant to spark the imagination of children, to transport them to a world where anything is possible, and to remind them of the power they hold within themselves – the power to dream, to create, and to tell their own stories.

Whether you're a seasoned reader revisiting the wonders of childhood or a young mind embarking on your own literary adventure, I invite you to step into the whispering woods and let your imagination take flight. Allow yourself to be captivated by the whimsical creatures and heartwarming tales, for within them lies a reminder of the magic that resides within us all.

Prologue

The humid summer air hung heavy with the scent of damp earth and wildflowers. Sunlight dappled through the canopy of ancient banyan trees, casting a mosaic of light and shadow on the dusty ground. Ten-year-old Hemlata crouched beneath the gnarled roots of the largest tree, her heart pounding with excitement and a touch of apprehension.

In her hand, a worn leather notebook held the key to her secret world. Its pages were filled with fantastical tales – talking squirrels with mischievous grins, wise old owls dispensing ancient wisdom, and a princess with fiery red hair who dreamt of adventures beyond the castle walls. These weren't just stories; they were Hemlata's escape, a refuge from the stifling expectations of her small village.

Hemlata wasn't supposed to be writing stories. In her world, girls were expected to learn household chores and prepare for marriage. Yet, the whispers of the woods, the rustling of leaves, and the symphony of buzzing insects fueled a fire within her – a fire that demanded expression.

This notebook was her sanctuary, a world where imagination reigned supreme and anything was possible.

Suddenly, a twig snapped beneath her, sending a jolt of fear through her. Heart hammering in her chest, Hemlata whipped her head around, her eyes scanning the shadowed undergrowth. A flicker of movement caught her eye – a flash of ginger fur disappearing behind a thick tree trunk.

Her fear subsided, replaced by a thrill of anticipation. Perhaps it was Pipsqueak, the mischievous squirrel who often featured in her stories, come to hear the latest adventure she had penned.

A mischievous smile lit up Hemlata's face. With newfound courage, she settled back against the tree trunk, her fingers tightening around the worn leather cover of her notebook. It was time to continue her story, to whisper secrets to the wind and let her imagination take flight in the magical world of "The Whispering Woods."

Acknowledgment

"The Whispering Woods" is a story inspired by the imagination of a fictional character named Hemlata. However, it is not intended to be a story written by Hemlata herself. It is an original creation by the author, (Mrigendra Bharti).

The author has drawn inspiration from Hemlata's life and imagination to create a story that transports readers to a world infused with Hemlata's childhood dreams and stories. To make Hemlata's character more relatable and realistic, the story incorporates themes and experiences inspired by real life.

The author wishes to remind readers that Hemlata is a fictional character, and the events depicted in the story are not factual.

The author would like to express gratitude to the following individuals and entities:

DISCLAIMER

This story is not affiliated with any person or entity in any way. The views and opinions expressed within are solely those of the author.

Thank You

Author

Mrigendra Bharti

About Sellbrochure Vymish Entertainment

Sellbrochure Vymish Entertainment, recognized as India's largest book publishing company, has made significant strides in ensuring its extensive collection of books reaches audiences across the global market. This rapid expansion is a testament to the company's dedication to disseminating knowledge and literature far beyond national borders. Central to its success is its affiliation with InkWhirl Media Networks, a reputable entity in the media and publication industry known for its innovative and strategic approaches. Within this network, InkWhirl Publication LLC operates as a vital division, further enhancing the company's capabilities and reach in the international market.

The visionary behind this enterprise is Mrigendra Bharti, the founder of Sellbrochure Vymish Entertainment. His foresight and passion for the literary world have been instrumental in steering the company towards remarkable growth and recognition. Under his leadership, Sellbrochure Vymish Entertainment has not only expanded its catalog but also established a strong presence in both domestic and international markets. Mrigendra Bharti's commitment to excellence and innovation has been a driving force in the company's journey, ensuring that it stays ahead of industry trends and meets the evolving needs of readers worldwide.

Sellbrochure Vymish Entertainment operates under the robust support of its parental organization, Mrigendra Bharti Group InfoTech. This affiliation provides the necessary resources and strategic guidance, enabling the publishing company to undertake ambitious projects and explore new markets. Mrigendra Bharti Group InfoTech's extensive experience in technology and information services has been a valuable asset, allowing Sellbrochure Vymish Entertainment to integrate advanced digital solutions in its operations, thereby enhancing its distribution capabilities and reader engagement.

Through relentless efforts and a commitment to quality, Sellbrochure Vymish Entertainment continues to break barriers and expand the reach of Indian literature globally. The company's diverse portfolio includes a wide range of genres, catering to different age groups and interests, thereby fostering a rich and inclusive reading culture. As it continues to innovate and grow, Sellbrochure Vymish Entertainment remains dedicated to its mission of making literature accessible to all, contributing significantly to the global literary landscape.

Connect With Mrigendra,
Thank you very much for choosing this book.
You can also connect with me on Instagram,
https://www.instagram.com/i_mrigendrabharti.official
With Love,
Mrigendra Bharti

Introduction

Welcome, dear reader, to a world where whispers turn into stories and imagination reigns supreme. Step into the enchanting realm of "The Whispering Woods," where talking animals share secrets with curious children and brave princesses defy societal expectations. This book is not simply a collection of tales; it's a portal back to the boundless creativity of childhood, a time when fantastical creatures filled the rustling leaves and courageous heroes whispered promises of adventure.

Hemlata, the author of these stories, wasn't always the renowned writer you'll meet later in her journey. In her youth, she was a young girl yearning to weave fantastical narratives under the shade of a giant banyan tree. Her dusty notebooks brimmed with stories of talking squirrels with mischievous grins, wise owls dispensing ancient wisdom, and a princess with fiery red hair longing for adventures beyond the confines of her castle. These tales were her escape, a refuge from the stifling expectations of her small village, where girls were not encouraged to chase literary dreams.

Driven by an unyielding passion for storytelling, Hemlata poured her heart and soul into her creations. These pages, filled with the unrefined joy of childhood imagination, hold a magic that transcends age. They are an invitation to reconnect with your inner child, a reminder that the power to dream, create, and tell your own stories resides within each of us.

Here, you'll embark on captivating journeys with Hemlata's characters. You'll meet Pipsqueak, the mischievous squirrel who becomes an unlikely companion on many adventures. You'll encounter the wise old owl, whose knowledge and cryptic proverbs offer guidance to those who seek it. And you'll meet the spirited princess, who challenges the status quo and inspires young readers to believe in their own strength and dreams.

Whether you're a seasoned reader seeking a nostalgic journey back to childhood or a young mind embarking on your own literary adventure, "The Whispering Woods" welcomes you with open arms. Prepare to be captivated by whimsical creatures, heartwarming tales, and a reminder of the magic that resides within the whispers of imagination. So, settle in, dear reader, and let your journey begin.

Chapter 1: The Blossoming of Love

The bustling streets of Ahmedabad were a familiar symphony to Hemlata. The honking rickshaws, the rhythmic chatter of vendors, and the aroma of freshly fried jalebis from the corner stall - it was a chaotic melody that resonated with the vibrancy of her youth. But today, amidst the usual hustle, a different tune played in her heart. A nervous flutter, a secret smile that tugged at the corners of her lips. Today, she was meeting Rahul.

Rahul wasn't just any boy; he was a constellation of dreams in Hemlata's sky. They had met a year ago at a literature conference, two souls drawn together by their love for poetry. Rahul, with his mop of unruly hair and eyes that held the depth of a thousand unspoken poems, had captivated Hemlata from the very first word. Their conversations flowed effortlessly, like verses weaving a beautiful narrative. He introduced her to forgotten classics and unearthed hidden gems in the world of literature, each recommendation a key unlocking a new chamber in her heart.

Hemlata, with her fiery spirit and a wit that could disarm a cynic, had become Rahul's muse. He found inspiration in her laughter, her passion for social work, and the way her eyes sparkled when she spoke about her dreams of becoming a writer. Their late-night conversations under the fairy lights strung across her balcony, exchanging dreams and aspirations, had blossomed into a silent understanding, a shared language that only they could comprehend.

Today, their usual haunt was a quaint bookstore tucked away in a bylane. Hemlata reached the bookstore, her heart hammering a frantic rhythm against her ribs. A blush crept up her cheeks as she spotted Rahul browsing the shelves, his brow furrowed in concentration. He looked up, and then, a slow smile spread across his face, mirroring the one on hers.

"Hemlata! You made it," he exclaimed, his voice warm and welcoming.

"Of course," she replied, trying to sound nonchalant, "wouldn't miss it for the world."

They walked through the aisles, their fingers brushing occasionally, sending a jolt of electricity through Hemlata. Rahul picked out a worn copy of Pablo Neruda's love poems, his eyes twinkling.

"Remember our discussion on 'Ode to Solitude'?" he asked, handing her the book.

Hemlata's smile widened. "How could I forget? You were saying it wasn't just about isolation, but also about finding a love so deep that it creates its own universe."

Rahul's gaze locked with hers, his voice a husky whisper. "And I believe we're creating our own universe, Hemlata, one filled with words and unspoken emotions."

Hemlata felt a blush creep up her neck. In that stolen moment, amidst the towering shelves and the scent of old paper, their universe seemed to shrink to just the two of them. As they continued browsing, stealing glances and sharing whispered jokes, Hemlata knew this wasn't just a love story blossoming between the pages of a book; it was an unwritten poem waiting to be penned by their hearts.

Hemlata cradled the worn copy of Neruda's poems in her hands, her heart brimming with a newfound emotion. Rahul's words echoed in her mind, creating a sweet symphony that drowned out the city's clamor. They spent hours at the bookstore, losing themselves in the world of literature and whispered secrets. Rahul recited a Pablo Neruda sonnet, his voice rich and captivating, sending shivers down Hemlata's spine. The poem spoke of a love that defied boundaries, a love that mirrored the unspoken yearning in their hearts.

As the afternoon sun dipped below the horizon, casting long shadows across the bookstore, they reluctantly decided to leave. Walking side-by-side, a comfortable silence settled between them, punctuated by stolen glances and nervous laughter. Hemlata, usually a chatterbox, found herself tongue-tied in Rahul's presence.

Every rustle of leaves, every honking rickshaw seemed to heighten her awareness of him, of the unspoken bond that thrummed between them.

They reached a park, a haven of tranquillity amidst the urban sprawl. The air was fragrant with the scent of night jasmine, and the gentle breeze carried the melody of crickets chirping. They found a secluded spot beneath a sprawling banyan tree, its ancient branches weaving a canopy overhead. Hemlata settled onto a weathered bench, her heart pounding a frantic tattoo against her ribs.

Rahul sat beside her, a respectful distance that felt both agonizing and necessary. He picked up a fallen twig and traced patterns in the dust, his brow furrowed in thought. Finally, he spoke, his voice barely a whisper.

"Hemlata," he began, his voice laced with nervous energy, "these past few months have been... the most incredible time of my life."

Hemlata felt a warmth bloom in her chest. "For me too, Rahul," she confessed, her voice barely above a murmur.

A smile tugged at the corners of Rahul's lips.

"Your passion for literature, your social conscience, the way your eyes light up when you talk about your dreams..." he trailed off, his gaze fixed on a distant point.

Hemlata knew exactly where he was going. "It's the same for you, Rahul," she interjected softly.

"Your love for words, your ability to see the beauty in the ordinary, the way you..." she faltered, her cheeks flushing crimson.

Rahul's gaze snapped back to her, his eyes reflecting a kaleidoscope of emotions. "The way you what, Hemlata?" he asked, his voice husky with anticipation.

Hemlata took a deep breath, gathering her courage. "The way you make me feel," she whispered, her voice trembling slightly.

A radiant smile lit up Rahul's face. He leaned closer, the space between them shrinking to a mere whisper. "Hemlata," he began, his voice a low rumble, "I think... I think I'm falling for you."

Hemlata's heart soared. The words she had longed to hear, the feelings she had harbored deep within, were finally out in the open. A tear welled up in her eye, tracing a glistening path down her cheek.

"I... I feel the same way, Rahul," she confessed, her voice thick with emotion.

In that moonlit park, beneath the watchful eyes of the stars, their unspoken feelings bloomed into a beautiful confession. The air crackled with unspoken promises, with a love that transcended words. They spent the next few hours talking, sharing dreams and aspirations, their laughter echoing through the stillness of the night. Time seemed to lose all meaning as they basked in the newfound glow of their love.

As the first rays of dawn painted the sky with streaks of orange and pink, they knew it was time to part ways. A bittersweet pang tugged at Hemlata's heart as she said goodbye to Rahul. But the memory of his touch, the warmth of his confession, lingered on, a sweet promise that brightened her day.

The following days were a whirlwind of stolen glances, shy smiles, and late-night text messages. Rahul's poems took on a new meaning, each verse brimming with a love that resonated deep within Hemlata's soul. They met frequently at the bookstore, their conversations evolving from discussions on literature to whispered secrets and stolen kisses under the dim glow of the reading lamps.

Their love story, born amidst the dusty shelves and the scent of old paper, blossomed into a vibrant reality. They found solace in each other's company, their connection deepening with each passing day. Hemlata, once guarded and cautious, began to trust Rahul with her vulnerabilities, her dreams, and her deepest fears. Rahul, in turn, found in Hemlata a kindred spirit, a muse who ignited his creativity and inspired him to be a better version of himself.

However, their budding love story existed in a bubble, a fragile sanctuary oblivious to the harsh realities of the world. Hemlata, despite her progressive views, was subconsciously aware of the societal norms that dictated love and marriage. Her parents, particularly her father, a stern and traditional man, held a tight leash on her life. The idea of dating, especially someone outside their social circle, was a forbidden notion in their conservative household.

One evening, as Hemlata was lost in a daydream, reminiscing about her stolen moments with Rahul, her father's booming voice shattered the tranquility. He stood at the doorway, his face etched with a frown, a copy of Hemlata's text messages clutched in his hand. Her heart plummeted, a cold dread settling in her stomach.

"Hemlata," he boomed, his voice laced with anger, "who is this Rahul you've been talking to?"

Hemlata's carefully constructed world came crashing down. Her palms grew slick with sweat, and a lump formed in her throat. She stammered, desperately searching for an explanation, but the truth hung heavy in the air. Her father's gaze was like a searing spotlight, stripping away her defenses.

Finally, under his relentless questioning, Hemlata confessed everything. She spoke about her meetings with Rahul, their shared love for literature, and the blossoming of their love. As the words tumbled out of her mouth, a flicker of fear danced in her eyes.

Her father listened stoically, his face an unreadable mask. But when she finished, a storm erupted. He launched into a tirade, his voice echoing through the room. He called Rahul names, belittled his background, and questioned his intentions.

Hemlata flinched with every harsh word, her heart breaking with each accusation.

"Love stories are for fairytales, Hemlata," he thundered. "You need to focus on your studies, on finding a suitable match within our community. This... this is just a childish infatuation."

Hemlata tried to reason with him, to explain the depth of her feelings for Rahul, but her words were lost in the cacophony of her father's disapproval. The argument ended with an ultimatum. Hemlata was forbidden from contacting Rahul or even mentioning his name. Her father confiscated her phone, a symbolic gesture of his control over her life.

Hemlata retreated to her room, a prisoner in her own home. Tears streamed down her face, blurring her vision. The future she had envisioned with Rahul, filled with shared dreams and whispered promises, seemed to vanish into thin air. A suffocating sense of helplessness engulfed her. How could she defy her father's orders? How could she continue her relationship with Rahul without his knowledge?

As the weight of her predicament pressed down on her, a flicker of determination ignited within Hemlata. She wouldn't let her father dictate her happiness. She would find a way to see Rahul, to fight for their love, even if it meant defying the boundaries set by her family. But the path ahead was uncertain, fraught with challenges and potential heartbreak. The love story that had bloomed so beautifully now faced its first real test.

Days turned into weeks, and the silence in Hemlata's life was deafening. Her phone remained confiscated, a constant reminder of her restricted freedom. Yet, the spark of defiance that had ignited within her refused to be extinguished. Hemlata spent her days lost in thought, searching for a way to reconnect with Rahul.

One afternoon, while sorting through old notebooks, she stumbled upon a hidden compartment in her desk drawer. Inside, nestled amongst forgotten treasures, was a small, worn mobile phone – a relic from her childhood. A surge of hope shot through her. This could be her lifeline, her secret channel to communicate with Rahul.

With trembling fingers, she charged the phone and managed to activate an old SIM card. The screen flickered to life, a dusty window to the outside world. Hemlata knew this was a risky move, but the thought of being completely cut off from Rahul was unbearable.

Later that night, under the cloak of darkness, Hemlata snuck out onto the balcony. The cool night air provided a welcome relief from the stifling atmosphere within her house. With a pounding heart, she dialed Rahul's number, praying he would answer.

After what felt like an eternity, his voice filled her ear, a wave of warmth washing over her. Relief and joy mingled with a tinge of apprehension as they spoke in hushed tones. Hemlata explained her situation, the fear of her father's wrath, and her determination to find a way to be together.

Rahul, ever the source of support, listened patiently. He assured her of his love and expressed his unwavering belief in their relationship. However, he cautioned against making any hasty decisions. He suggested they bide their time, for a forceful rebellion could backfire spectacularly.

"We need a plan, Hemlata," he said, his voice firm yet gentle. "Something that won't arouse suspicion but allows us to stay connected."

A hesitant smile touched Hemlata's lips. The idea of a plan, however vague, instilled a sense of hope. They discussed possibilities, brainstorming ways to exchange messages without raising her father's doubts. Finally, they settled on a code – a series of seemingly mundane book titles mentioned in casual conversation with a friend, which Rahul could decipher.

The conversation ended with a promise – a promise to fight for their love, to find a way to be together despite the obstacles. As Hemlata hung up the phone, a newfound determination coursed through her veins. She wouldn't let her father's disapproval extinguish the flame of love that burned so brightly within her.

The next morning, Hemlata approached her friend Priya, a kindred spirit with a rebellious streak. Under the guise of seeking recommendations for an upcoming literature project, Hemlata subtly dropped the codewords –

"One Hundred Years of Solitude" and "Pride and Prejudice." Priya, quick to understand, winked conspiratorially.

Hemlata knew the road ahead wouldn't be easy. There would be arguments, anxieties, and the constant fear of discovery. But for the first time since her father's intervention, a spark of hope flickered within her. She had a plan, a secret connection to Rahul, and a newfound determination to fight for their love. The fight for their happily ever after had just begun.

Chapter 2: The Weight of Expectations

Months passed, blurring into a routine of stolen glances, coded messages, and whispered dreams. Hemlata navigated the treacherous waters of her double life with a newfound confidence. Her secret phone, hidden within a compartment in her mathematics textbook, became a lifeline to Rahul, a portal to the world of shared dreams that existed beyond her father's control.

Hemlata's relationship with her family, however, remained strained. Her father's disapproval hung heavy in the air, a constant reminder of the battle she was waging. He scrutinized her every move, his suspicion a dark cloud that loomed over her.

Hemlata learned to navigate his watchful eyes, her conversations meticulously crafted to avoid any mention of Rahul or their clandestine communication.

The pressure to conform to societal expectations intensified. Rishta meetings, once a distant worry, became a frequent occurrence. Hemlata was paraded before a series of suitable boys, each a carefully chosen match based on caste, social standing, and financial stability. Every meeting was an ordeal, a suffocating performance where she had to play the part of the ideal daughter, the perfect bride-to-be.

One sweltering afternoon, Hemlata found herself seated across from another prospective groom. This time, it was Amit, a young businessman, his family friends with her own. Amit, with his neatly combed hair and designer clothes, exuded an air of arrogance that grated on Hemlata's nerves. Their conversation was a series of polite exchanges devoid of any real connection.

Hemlata felt like a character in a play, mouthing lines she didn't believe in.

As the afternoon progressed, Amit's parents began a subtle interrogation, probing for details about Hemlata's education, her hobbies, and her expectations from married life. Hemlata answered their questions politely, but her mind wandered to Rahul. She yearned to be discussing literature, dissecting poems, and sharing dreams, not discussing ideal household chores and the perfect dinner menu.

When the meeting finally concluded, Hemlata felt drained. As she walked alongside her mother, she couldn't hold back any longer. "Ma," she began, a hesitant tone lacing her voice, "how long will this charade continue?"

Her mother, a silent observer throughout the ordeal, sighed. "Hemlata, beta," she said, her voice soft yet firm, "you know this is how things are done. You need to find a suitable match, someone who will take care of you and build a good life."

Frustration bubbled within Hemlata. "But what about love, Ma? What about finding someone I connect with on an intellectual and emotional level?"

Her mother's gaze softened, a flicker of sadness crossing her eyes. "Love, Hemlata," she said, her voice barely a whisper, "is a luxury we can't all afford. Marriage is about stability, about building a future together. Love can come later, with time."

Hemlata felt a knot tighten in her chest. The weight of her mother's words, though unspoken, was clear – her dreams of a love story based on shared passions and genuine connection were nothing more than a fantasy. Her parents, bound by tradition and societal pressures, couldn't comprehend the depth of her feelings for Rahul.

As the days turned into weeks, Hemlata's frustration grew. The constant pressure to conform, the never-ending string of Rishta meetings, and the stifling control of her father created a suffocating sense of confinement. She found solace only in her stolen moments with Rahul, their coded messages a secret language that kept their love alive.

One rainy evening, as Hemlata sat huddled under a blanket, a message from Rahul arrived. It was an excerpt from a poem by William Butler Yeats, a poem they had both admired. But this time, the message held a hidden meaning, a code they had developed to discuss more serious matters. It was a call for action, a suggestion to meet in person.

Hemlata's heart pounded with a mixture of excitement and fear. The thought of seeing Rahul, of feeling his touch and hearing his voice after what felt like an eternity, was exhilarating. But the risk of discovery, the potential consequences of defying her father's orders, were as terrifying as they were real. Yet, a fierce determination to fight for their love burned brighter than ever.

Hemlata spent the next few days in a whirlwind of nervous anticipation. The prospect of meeting Rahul, a secret rendezvous defying her father's control, sent shivers down her spine. The excitement of seeing him was tempered by the fear of getting caught, of the potential fallout that could jeopardize their relationship and her future.

She knew she needed a plan, a way to slip out of the house undetected. Rahul, ever the resourceful one, suggested utilizing the annual Diwali celebrations as a cover. Diwali, the festival of lights, was a time for vibrant festivities, elaborate decorations, and countless family visits. It was the perfect opportunity for Hemlata to create a window of escape.

The days leading up to Diwali were a blur of preparations. Hemlata helped her mother decorate the house with strings of twinkling lights and colorful rangolis. The festive spirit filled the air, but Hemlata's heart remained heavy with worry. She had to ensure her escape went

unnoticed, to avoid raising any suspicion.

Finally, the night of Diwali arrived. The house buzzed with activity as relatives streamed in, exchanging greetings and sharing sweets.

Hemlata, dressed in a dazzling lehenga, went through the motions, her smile strained and her eyes scanning the crowd for an opportunity. The cacophony of laughter and firecrackers created a perfect cover for her plan.

When her aunt, usually glued to her side during such gatherings, got engrossed in a conversation with a neighbor, Hemlata seized her chance.

With a quick excuse about needing some fresh air, she slipped out onto the balcony. Her heart pounded in her chest as she dialed Rahul's number.

"I'm outside," she whispered into the phone, her voice barely audible above the din of festivities.

Relief flooded her voice as she heard Rahul's response. "I'm on my way," he said, his voice filled with urgency.

Minutes felt like hours as Hemlata paced nervously on the balcony. The flickering flames of diyas cast long shadows, and the air crackled with a nervous energy. Just as despair began to creep in, she spotted a familiar figure across the street, weaving through the crowd.

Rahul, disguised with a cap pulled low over his forehead, reached the balcony. Hemlata's breath hitched in her throat. It was the first time they had seen each other in months, and the sight of him filled her with an overwhelming sense of relief and joy.

Their meeting, however, was far from a romantic rendezvous. The balcony, bathed in the soft glow of a single diya, provided a precarious perch for their stolen conversation. Rahul, his voice hushed, explained his plan. He had secured a place at a prestigious university outside the city, pursuing a Master's degree in literature.

"Hemlata," he said, his gaze intense, "I believe this is our chance. We can escape the confines of this city, the expectations of our families.

Come with me, let's build a life together where we can pursue our dreams and be true to ourselves."

The idea of leaving everything behind, of defying her family's expectations, was both exhilarating and terrifying. Hemlata looked into Rahul's eyes, her heart overflowing with love and a yearning for a future together. She knew this decision would have far-reaching consequences, potentially straining relationships and jeopardizing her future. Yet, the thought of living a life devoid of love and freedom was unbearable.

"Give me some time," Hemlata whispered, her voice trembling slightly. "I need to think, to weigh my options."

Rahul understood. He squeezed her hand gently, his touch sending a jolt of electricity through her.

"Think carefully, Hemlata," he said, his voice filled with a quiet determination. "But know this, no matter what you decide, my love for you remains unchanged."

With that, he turned and disappeared into the throng of people, leaving Hemlata alone on the balcony, the weight of his proposal and the burden of her choice heavy on her heart. As the celebrations continued within the house, Hemlata stood amidst the flickering lights, facing a crossroads in her life. Would she choose love and freedom, defying her family's expectations?

Or would she succumb to societal pressures, sacrificing her dreams for a life of tradition and conformity?

The Diwali night stretched into a blur of emotions for Hemlata. Sleep eluded her. She tossed and turned in bed, the weight of Rahul's proposal pressing down on her chest. The flickering image of his hopeful eyes intertwined with the disapproving face of her father, creating a storm within her.

Love, with its fiery intensity, beckoned her towards freedom. The prospect of escaping the suffocating confines of her life, of pursuing her dreams alongside Rahul in a new city, filled her with a sense of liberation. His words resonated deep within her, promising a future where their shared passion for literature could flourish, unbound by societal constraints.

But the path of love was fraught with thorns. Leaving everything behind, severing ties with her family, was a daunting proposition. The guilt of potentially causing her parents, especially her mother, immense pain gnawed at her conscience. Leaving them behind felt like betraying their love and sacrifices for her well-being.

Hemlata knew her decision would have far-reaching consequences. Her father's fury was predictable, the potential ostracization from the community a harsh reality. Yet, the thought of a life devoid of love, of marrying someone she barely knew, felt like a fate worse than exile.

The following days were a blur of forced conversations and a strained silence within the household. Diwali celebrations faded, leaving behind an emptiness that mirrored the one in Hemlata's heart. She found solace in stolen moments with Rahul, their coded messages carrying the weight of their unspoken anxieties.

One evening, Hemlata sought refuge in her favorite corner of the local library. Surrounded by the comforting scent of old paper and the reassuring silence, she poured her heart out in a letter to Rahul. She spoke of her love for him, the yearning for a life together, but also confessed her fears – the fear of hurting her family, the uncertainty of a future built on defiance.

Days later, a reply arrived, scrawled in Rahul's familiar handwriting. His words were a balm to her troubled soul. He acknowledged her fears and anxieties, but also emphasized his unwavering love and support. He offered a solution, a compromise that could potentially bridge the gap between love and family.

They could elope, a simple ceremony witnessed by a few close friends. While this wouldn't appease her father, it wouldn't be a complete rejection of tradition. With time, perhaps, he would come to accept their decision. But the key was for Hemlata to be strong, to believe in their love and fight for their future.

Hemlata reread the letter several times, weighing Rahul's suggestion in her mind. Elopement felt like a gamble, a risky move that could either pave the way for their happiness or further fracture her relationship with her family. Yet, the thought of forever losing Rahul, of leading a life devoid of love, was unbearable.

As the days turned into weeks, a quiet determination settled over Hemlata. She knew what she had to do. It wouldn't be easy, there would be hardships and tears, but she wouldn't let fear dictate her future. She yearned for a life filled with love, freedom, and the pursuit of her dreams – a life she could only build with Rahul by her side.

With a deep breath, Hemlata picked up the phone, her heart pounding a frantic rhythm. She had a decision to make, a choice that would alter the course of her life. It was time to call Rahul and tell him her answer. The weight of expectations, both societal and personal, hung heavy on her heart, but she was finally ready to take a stand for her love and her future.

Hemlata's hand trembled slightly as she dialed Rahul's number. The weeks of indecision and internal conflict had culminated in this moment.

As the phone rang, a thousand emotions warred within her – fear of her father's wrath, the guilt of potentially hurting her family, and the overwhelming desire to be with Rahul.

Finally, his voice, warm and familiar, filled the line. "Hemlata?" he said, a hint of anxiety lacing his tone.

Taking a deep breath, Hemlata plunged into it.

"Rahul," she began, her voice barely a whisper, "I've read your letter multiple times. I've spent days agonizing over it, weighing my options, and..." she faltered, her heart pounding against her ribs.

"And?" Rahul prompted, his voice a mix of hope and trepidation.

"And," Hemlata continued, a new resolve hardening her voice, "I agree. We elope."

A gasp escaped from Rahul's end. The silence stretched for a moment, thick with emotion. Then, a joyous laugh erupted, a sound that echoed Hemlata's own burgeoning sense of relief and exhilaration.

"Hemlata! Are you serious?" he exclaimed, his voice brimming with disbelief and happiness.

"Absolutely," she declared, a newfound confidence filling her voice. "I can't live without you, and I refuse to let fear dictate my future. I want to build a life with you, Rahul, a life filled with love, freedom, and the pursuit of our dreams."

Their conversation continued late into the night. They discussed the logistics of their daring plan – arranging the marriage certificate, booking train tickets to the city where Rahul's university was located, and informing a few trusted friends who would serve as witnesses.

The following days were a whirlwind of activity. Hemlata managed to sneak out a few essential belongings – clothes, a treasured collection of poetry books, and a photograph of her mother tucked inside her diary. It was a heartbreaking act, taking only what she could carry, leaving behind the life she knew.

As the day of their elopement arrived, Hemlata felt a mix of excitement and nervousness gnaw at her stomach. It was a day of goodbyes and new beginnings. Under the cover of twilight, they met at their usual rendezvous spot - the park beneath the banyan tree. This time, however, it wasn't a stolen conversation but a momentous step towards their future.

With the help of their friends, they secured a taxi and sped towards the railway station. Leaving Ahmedabad behind, they hurtled towards a future filled with uncertainty, yet brimming with the promise of love and freedom. Their journey was just beginning, and the challenges of defying societal norms and gaining acceptance from their families loomed large.

But as Hemlata glanced at Rahul, his hand intertwined with hers, a feeling of peace washed over her. They were in this together, two souls united by their love for literature and their unwavering commitment to their dreams. They had taken a daring leap of faith, leaving behind the confines of tradition to build their own story, a love story written in defiance and chased with the ink of courage. They were on their way to a city far away, where a new chapter, filled with love and the promise of a life together, awaited them.

Chapter 3: A New Dawn in a City of Dreams

The rhythmic clatter of the train lulled Hemlata into a restless sleep. Dreams, both vivid and fleeting, flickered through her mind – images of her childhood home, her tearful mother's face, and Rahul's unwavering gaze. The weight of her decision, the act of defiance against her family's expectations, settled heavily on her heart. Yet, interwoven with the anxiety was a glimmer of hope, a newfound freedom that pulsed through her veins.

As dawn painted the sky with streaks of pink and orange, the train pulled into the bustling city station of their new beginning. The air was thick with the sounds of honking vehicles and the cacophony of a vibrant metropolis, a stark contrast to the quiet life Hemlata had left behind. Stepping off the train, hand in hand with Rahul, she felt a mix of excitement and trepidation.

The city, a sprawling mass of concrete and glass, was a far cry from the familiar streets of Ahmedabad. Towering skyscrapers scraped the sky, and the chaotic dance of traffic seemed endless. Yet, amidst the urban chaos, Hemlata sensed a certain energy, a pulse of possibilities that resonated with her yearning for a new life.

Their first task was to find a place to stay. Rahul, having arrived a few weeks earlier to secure his university accommodation, had a temporary room in a modest boarding house not far from the bustling university campus. The room, though small and simple, offered a haven from the city's clamor. It was here, amidst the stacks of unpacked books and scattered belongings, that they began to build their new life together.

The initial days were a blur of adjustments and unfamiliar routines. Hemlata, used to the comfort of her family home, struggled with the daily chores of cooking and managing a small budget. The city lights, which had initially seemed exciting, now felt intrusive, disrupting her sleep patterns. Yet, Rahul's unwavering support and his gentle humor made the transition easier.

Together, they explored the city, venturing into bustling markets, hidden alleyways adorned with street art, and quaint cafes that served steaming cups of chai and delicious samosas. In these explorations, Hemlata discovered a new city, not just of towering buildings and honking vehicles, but a city brimming with artistic energy, hidden historical gems, and a vibrant student life that mirrored her own youthful spirit.

Their days were filled with new experiences.

Hemlata sat in on Rahul's literature classes, fascinated by the lively discussions and in-depth analysis of her favorite poems. She enrolled in a short writing workshop at the university, a chance to rekindle her passion for storytelling and discover a new voice amidst the anonymity of the city. Slowly, a sense of belonging began to take root within her.

However, the joy of their new life was tempered by the ever-present shadow of their decision.

Communication with Hemlata's family remained a delicate issue. A single phone call, intercepted by her father, could shatter their fragile peace.

Messages exchanged through mutual friends were cryptic and anxiety-inducing. Hemlata yearned for a reconciliation with her mother, a longing for her understanding and love.

One evening, as they sat on the rooftop of their boarding house, gazing at the twinkling city lights, Hemlata poured out her heart to Rahul. "I miss my mother terribly, Rahul," she confessed, her voice choked with emotion. "I know I defied her wishes, but a part of me longs for her acceptance, for a bridge between us."

Rahul understood. He pulled her close, his embrace a silent source of comfort. "We'll find a way, Hemlata," he assured her. "Perhaps with time, they'll come to understand our love. And your mother, she loves you dearly, I'm sure of it.

Maybe with a letter, a heartfelt explanation..."

His words offered a glimmer of hope. That night, Hemlata penned a long letter to her mother, pouring out her feelings, explaining the reasons behind her decision, and expressing her unwavering love and respect. It was a plea for understanding, a bridge built with words and tears, in the hope that it might reach her mother's heart.

As weeks turned into months, Hemlata and Rahul settled into a rhythm in their new life. The city, once overwhelming, became a familiar friend. Their love story, born amidst stolen glances and whispered poems, blossomed in this new environment. They attended poetry readings together, discussing their interpretations with a newfound passion. Rahul, inspired by Hemlata's determination, began writing short stories, finding his own voice in the vast world of literature.

One sunny afternoon, while browsing through a bookstore, Hemlata stumbled upon a flyer announcing a literary competition. The theme, "Love in the Time of Defiance," resonated deeply with her. A spark ignited within her, an urge to tell their story, their unconventional love story that had defied societal norms.

With Rahul's encouragement ringing in her ears, Hemlata decided to enter the literary competition. The theme, "Love in the Time of Defiance," resonated deeply with her. It was an opportunity to tell their story, their unconventional love story that had defied societal norms, a tale woven with the threads of longing, courage, and unwavering love.

Night after night, Hemlata poured her experiences onto the page. She crafted a narrative that weaved through the familiar streets of Ahmedabad, the hushed meetings under the banyan tree, the exhilarating train journey, and the challenges of their new life in the city. It was a poignant tale of love and defiance, a testament to the strength of their bond and their unwavering belief in their future.

Hemlata's writing sessions became a nightly ritual. Rahul, her biggest supporter, would sit beside her, offering feedback and sharing his own writing endeavors. Their nights were filled not just with the clatter of keyboards but also with the spark of creativity and the joy of shared dreams.

One evening, as Hemlata worked on her story, a wave of loneliness washed over her. She missed the warmth of family gatherings, the playful banter with her siblings, and the comforting presence of her mother. Tears welled up in her eyes, blurring the words on the screen.

Rahul, sensing her distress, pulled her close.

"Hemlata," he whispered, his voice gentle, "It's alright to miss them. But don't let it cloud your happiness. They will come around, in time."

He was right. The pain of estrangement wouldn't disappear overnight, but Hemlata knew she couldn't let it hold her back. She had a story to tell, a future to build, and a love to cherish. With renewed determination, she pushed on, finishing her manuscript just in time for the competition deadline.

Weeks turned into months, and the news of the competition results arrived. Hemlata's heart pounded in her chest as she ripped open the envelope. Disappointment stabbed at her as her eyes scanned the first page, devoid of her name. But then, at the very bottom, nestled amongst the honorable mentions, it was there - "Hemlata Patel."

An unexpected surge of joy filled her. While she hadn't won the competition, the recognition, the

validation of her story, was a victory in itself.

More importantly, it instilled in her a newfound confidence in her writing abilities. This could be a beginning, a stepping stone to a future where her love for literature wasn't just a secret passion, but a pursuit she could share with the world.

The news spread quickly within the university's literary circle. Hemlata found herself invited to open mic nights and discussions with established authors. Her story, shared in fragments at these events, resonated with many students, particularly those navigating unconventional love stories or facing societal pressures. Hemlata realized her story wasn't just hers; it was a shared experience, a tale of love and defiance that resonated with a generation seeking to carve their own paths.

One evening, after a particularly successful reading session, a woman approached Hemlata. Her warm smile and kind eyes held a familiarity that sent a tremor of hope through Hemlata. The woman introduced herself as Dr. Verma, a professor of literature at the university and a judge for the writing competition.

"Your story, Ms. Patel," Dr. Verma began, her voice filled with admiration, "it was truly a breath of fresh air. It touched me deeply, the courage you displayed, the strength of your love. Hemlata, have you considered pursuing writing further?"

Hemlata's breath hitched. The possibility, once a forbidden dream, felt closer than ever. Dr. Verma offered her guidance, suggesting writing workshops and mentorship opportunities within the university. It was a chance to hone her craft, to learn from established authors, and potentially find a path towards publication.

As Hemlata walked home that evening, hand in hand with Rahul, a renewed sense of excitement bubbled within her. They had faced challenges, defied expectations, and built a life together.

Now, with her writing gaining recognition, a future filled with literary pursuits seemed within reach. But the most important aspect of her journey remained unchanged - her love for Rahul, a love that had blossomed amidst defiance and had become the bedrock of their extraordinary story.

Months passed in a flurry of activity. Hemlata, under Dr. Verma's watchful guidance, began attending writing workshops and seminars. She immersed herself in the world of literature, devouring novels, analyzing poems, and actively participating in discussions. The once-shy girl who found solace in stolen moments with books now blossomed into a confident young woman, her voice finding its strength among a community that shared her passion.

Rahul, her constant source of support, thrived in his own academic pursuits. His short stories, imbued with a touch of magical realism, began garnering attention from his professors. Their evenings, once filled with anxieties about their future, were now spent reading each other's work, offering constructive criticism, and celebrating each other's successes.

One afternoon, while browsing through the university library, Hemlata stumbled upon a familiar face. It was Priya, her childhood friend and confidante. An unexpected wave of joy washed over her. Priya, after completing her studies, had secured a job in the same city. The reunion was filled with laughter, shared stories, and a heartfelt exchange of news.

Hemlata confided in Priya about her new life, her budding writing career, and the lingering estrangement with her family. Priya, ever the empathetic friend, listened patiently and promised to help mend bridges.

A few days later, Priya presented Hemlata with a small box wrapped in colorful paper. Inside, nestled amongst dried rose petals, lay a delicate silver bracelet adorned with a familiar charm – a miniature banyan tree, a symbol of their secret meetings in Ahmedabad. Priya explained that she had contacted Hemlata's mother, conveying her well-being and expressing her desire for reconciliation.

Tears welled up in Hemlata's eyes. This small token, a symbol of her childhood home and her mother's love, was a glimmer of hope. That night, with trembling hands, she penned another letter to her mother, not filled with justifications or accusations, but with simple expressions of love and longing for a connection, a bridge built with vulnerability and a daughter's yearning for her mother's understanding.

Days turned into weeks, and the silence stretched on. Hemlata's hope began to dwindle, replaced by a familiar ache of loneliness. Then, one morning, a knock on their boarding house door shattered the silence. Standing there, her eyes filled with a mixture of apprehension and longing, was Hemlata's mother.

The reunion was filled with tears and unspoken

words. Hemlata's mother, her face etched with worry, embraced Hemlata tightly, the warmth of her touch a balm on Hemlata's yearning heart.

Over steaming cups of chai, Hemlata shared stories of their new life, of Rahul's support, and her newfound passion for writing.

Her mother listened intently, the disapproval in her eyes replaced by a flicker of understanding.

Hemlata's courage, her pursuit of happiness, and her success in the literary world chipped away at the walls of tradition that had initially separated them.

The visit was short, a tentative step towards

reconciliation. Yet, it marked a turning point in their relationship. Hemlata's mother, before leaving, gifted her a tattered copy of Rabindranath Tagore's poems, a book they used to read together when Hemlata was a child. It was a silent gesture of acceptance, a bridge built on shared memories and the enduring bond between a mother and daughter.

News of the visit spread quickly within Hemlata's family. Soon, a call came from her father. His voice, though gruff, held a hint of warmth as he inquired about her well-being. It was a small step, a crack in the wall of his disapproval, offering a glimmer of hope for a future reconciliation.

As Hemlata hung up the phone, a sense of peace settled over her. The journey had been arduous, fraught with challenges and uncertainties. But with unwavering love, defiance, and the pursuit of her dreams, she had built a new life for herself, a life where love and literature intertwined. The future remained uncertain, but Hemlata faced it with her head held high, her heart brimming with hope, and the promise of a love story that defied tradition and bloomed into a testament to courage and resilience.

Years flowed by, etching themselves onto the canvas of Hemlata and Rahul's life. Their tiny boarding house room had been replaced by a cozy apartment, filled with bookshelves overflowing with cherished novels and their own published works. Hemlata's name was no longer confined to competition mentions; it graced the covers of literary magazines and the spines of critically acclaimed novels. Her stories, inspired by her love for Rahul and their unconventional journey, resonated with readers across the country.

Hemlata and Rahul, a literary power couple, had become synonymous with defying societal norms and pursuing love. Their story, once whispered under the banyan tree, now unfolded in their novels, captivating audiences and sparking conversations about love, tradition, and the courage to follow one's heart.

Their apartment became a haven for budding writers, a place where Hemlata, under the tutelage of Dr. Verma who had become a close friend, hosted workshops and offered guidance to aspiring authors. Rahul, too, found success. His short stories, imbued with a touch of magical realism, evolved into a captivating novel that explored the themes of identity and the complexities of human relationships.

One evening, as they sat on their balcony overlooking the bustling city, their hands intertwined, Hemlata turned to Rahul, a radiant smile illuminating her face. "Remember that night we ran away on the train?" she asked, her voice tinged with a touch of nostalgia.

Rahul chuckled, a warm light dancing in his eyes.

"How could I forget? It was the night we embarked on the greatest adventure of our lives."

They reminisced about their initial struggles, their anxieties, and the joy of finding acceptance from their families. Hemlata's father, though initially hesitant, had eventually visited them in the city, a silent apology conveyed through his gruff gestures and tear-filled eyes. Her mother remained a constant source of support, her visits filled with warm hugs and whispered words of encouragement.

As the stars twinkled above them, Hemlata confessed, "You know, Rahul, without your love and unwavering support, none of this would have been possible."

Rahul leaned in, his lips brushing against her ear.

"And without your courage and determination, our love story wouldn't have a platform to inspire others. We did it together, Hemlata."

Their journey had been one of defiance, love, and unwavering pursuit of dreams. They had defied societal expectations, carved their own path, and emerged stronger, their love story a symphony of success.

Looking ahead, their future glittered with possibilities. Hemlata was working on a new novel, a story about a young woman's journey of self-discovery set against the backdrop of a vibrant city. Rahul, inspired by their experiences, was venturing into the world of screenwriting, hoping to translate their story onto the silver screen.

Hemlata and Rahul, their love story forever etched in ink and memory, knew that their journey was far from over. New challenges awaited, fresh adventures beckoned, and the world of literature, their shared passion, was their canvas upon which they would continue to paint their love story for the world to see and celebrate.

Chapter 4: Echoes of the Past

Five years had passed since Hemlata and Rahul had embarked on their daring escape to the city of dreams. Their once tiny boarding house room had transformed into a haven for creativity.

Sunlight streamed through the expansive windows, illuminating bookshelves overflowing with cherished novels and their own published works. Trophies and awards adorned a corner table, testaments to their literary achievements.

Hemlata, her name now synonymous with captivating narratives and raw emotional exploration, sat nestled in her favorite armchair, furiously tapping away at her keyboard. Her brow furrowed in concentration, her fingers danced across the keys, weaving a story that promised to be even more poignant than her previous ones.

This time, the protagonist wasn't a reflection of herself, but a nuanced exploration of her mother's perspective – a journey of acceptance and understanding.

The inspiration for this new project had struck unexpectedly. A phone call from her father, his voice gruff yet filled with a tremor of emotion, had revealed a hidden truth. Her mother, ever the pillar of strength, had been diagnosed with a critical illness. The news ripped through Hemlata, a stark reminder of the precious time that could slip away if left unaddressed.

Hemlata yearned to understand her mother's journey, the silent battles fought within the confines of tradition, and the sacrifices made in the name of family. With this new story, she hoped to bridge the distance that remained, to weave a tale of reconciliation and unspoken love between a mother and daughter.

A notification on her laptop screen broke her concentration. It was an email from Rahul, her ever-supportive partner. He was attending a film festival in a nearby city, his screenplay based on their love story nominated for an award.

Hemlata's heart swelled with pride. Their journey, once shrouded in secrecy and defiance, was now being celebrated on a public platform.

Their love story, a testament to courage and unwavering passion, had transcended the pages of their novels. It resonated with readers and aspiring writers who found inspiration in their defiance of tradition. Hemlata and Rahul, their love story a living testament to their beliefs, often hosted workshops and talks, offering guidance and encouragement to those who dared to pursue unconventional paths.

The following day, Hemlata found herself on a train, the rhythmic clatter echoing the journey she took years ago with Rahul. This time, however, the destination was different. It was a small town nestled amidst rolling hills, a place where memories of her childhood home and the life she left behind resided.

Stepping off the train, Hemlata was greeted by the familiar scent of mango trees and the cacophony of street vendors. The bustling streets, once a world away, now felt strangely alien. As she navigated her way back to her childhood home, a wave of emotions washed over her – nostalgia, apprehension, and a yearning for the warmth she had once known.

The house remained the same, a comforting presence amidst the changing world. Yet, an air of melancholy hung over it. Her father, his face etched with worry, greeted her with a strained embrace. The once-vibrant spark in his eyes had dimmed, replaced by a quiet sadness.

Inside, the house felt empty. The silence was deafening, punctuated only by the rhythmic hum of the old ceiling fan. Hemlata learned from her father that her mother was too weak to make the journey to the city, choosing to spend her remaining days in the familiar comfort of their home.

The news hit Hemlata like a punch in the gut.

Tears welled up in her eyes, a torrent of emotions threatening to spill over. Hemlata spent the next few days by her mother's bedside, reading her favorite poems, sharing stories from her life in the city, and simply being present. There were no apologies, no justifications. Just a quiet understanding settling between them, a bond rekindled through shared moments and the unspoken language of love.

One afternoon, as Hemlata read a passage from her new novel, her mother reached for her hand, a weak smile gracing her lips. "It's beautiful, Hemlata," she whispered, her voice hoarse but filled with a flicker of pride. "You've captured the heart of a woman caught between tradition and her child's happiness."

Tears streamed down Hemlata's cheeks. It wasn't just the story resonating with her mother; it was their own shared journey, reflected in the pages of the book. The distance, the years of estrangement, began to melt away, replaced by a profound understanding and a deep love that transcended unspoken words.

Hemlata stayed by her mother's side for the next few weeks, cherishing each stolen moment. They spoke of the past, not with blame or anger, but with a newfound acceptance. Her mother shared stories of Hemlata's childhood, her quiet strength, and her insatiable love for stories.

Hemlata, in turn, shared her experiences in the city, the challenges faced, and the triumphs achieved.

One evening, as the sun dipped below the horizon, painting the sky in hues of orange and pink, Hemlata held her mother's hand, her heart heavy with a love that transcended words. "Maa," she began, her voice trembling slightly, "I'm so grateful for your love and understanding."

Her mother squeezed her hand weakly.

"Hemlata," she whispered, her voice barely a breath, "you followed your dreams, your heart. I may not have understood at first, but I'm proud of the woman you've become."

Those words, a culmination of years of unspoken emotions, were a balm to Hemlata's soul. The weight of her decision, the years of estrangement, lifted a little. A tear rolled down her cheek, landing on her mother's frail hand.

Days turned into weeks, and the inevitable drew closer. One morning, Hemlata woke to a stillness in the room. Panic surged through her as she rushed to her mother's bedside. Her father, eyes red-rimmed with grief, stood beside the bed, a silent confirmation of their loss.

Hemlata held her mother's hand, her body wracked with sobs. Grief threatened to consume her, but through the haze of tears, a sense of gratitude emerged. The final weeks spent together had been a gift, a chance to mend bridges and express the love that had always existed between them, even amidst the turmoil.

The days following the funeral were a blur of rituals and mourning. The familiar comfort of her childhood home now felt suffocating, filled with the echoes of her mother's laughter and the warmth of her presence. Bidding farewell to her father, a man forever changed by grief, Hemlata boarded the train back to the city, carrying with her a legacy of love and a story waiting to be told.

Back in their cozy apartment, surrounded by the familiar comfort of their shared space, Rahul enveloped Hemlata in a hug, his presence a silent source of strength. He had returned from the film festival, his achievement overshadowed by the news of Hemlata's loss.

The next few weeks were shrouded in a cloak of sadness. Hemlata found solace in writing, pouring her grief and the memories of her mother onto the page. The unfinished novel became a poignant tribute, a conversation with her mother that transcended the boundaries of life and death.

As Hemlata immersed herself in writing, Rahul worked tirelessly on revising his screenplay. The award he received at the film festival had opened doors, and now, the possibility of their love story being depicted on the silver screen loomed large.

One evening, as they sat on their balcony, the city lights twinkling below, Hemlata glanced at Rahul. "We should visit Ahmedabad again," she proposed, her voice laced with a hint of melancholy.

Rahul understood. A visit to their childhood home, the banyan tree, and the streets they once walked secretly held the power of healing and closure. They planned their trip, their shared memories acting as a guide.

The journey back to Ahmedabad was bittersweet. As they stood beneath the same banyan tree where their love story began, years seemed to melt away. Memories flooded back – stolen glances, whispered promises, and the exhilarating fear of their elopement.

Hemlata placed a hand on the rough bark, a silent tribute to the love that had blossomed under its shade. Tears welled up in her eyes, but this time, they were not just tears of grief. They were tears of gratitude for the love that had sustained her, the courage it had instilled, and the story it had birthed.

Returning from Ahmedabad, a renewed sense of purpose settled within Hemlata. Her mother's passing, while a devastating loss, had ignited a burning desire to finish the novel – a story that paid homage to her mother's love and sacrifice.

As she poured her heart onto the page, the unfinished manuscript transformed into a powerful testament to a mother-daughter bond, navigating tradition and evolving love.

Meanwhile, Rahul's career experienced a meteoric rise. His screenplay, a poignant adaptation of their love story, garnered critical acclaim and secured the backing of a prestigious production house. The prospect of their journey translating into a film, captivating audiences on a larger scale, filled them with a mix of excitement and apprehension.

The following months were a whirlwind of activity. Hemlata, her novel nearing completion, juggled writing sessions with promotional interviews for her previous works. Rahul, collaborating with the film director, delved into the intricate world of filmmaking, ensuring their story retained its authenticity.

One evening, amidst the chaos, Hemlata stumbled upon a dusty box while cleaning out a forgotten corner of their apartment. Inside, she found a collection of her childhood writings – poems, short stories, and unfinished drafts. A forgotten dream, a faint echo of a young girl who yearned to be a writer, flickered back to life.

Hemlata spent the following days sifting through her childhood creations, a wave of nostalgia washing over her. These stories, filled with an innocent charm and unbridled imagination, were a testament to her lifelong passion for storytelling. Holding them in her hand, she realized her journey as a writer wasn't just about defiance or achieving success. It was about a calling, a voice that had always resided within her, nurtured by stolen moments with books and the solace found within the written word.

Inspired by this rediscovery, Hemlata began dedicating a portion of her time to revisiting her childhood writings. She started rewriting some of the stories, injecting them with the maturity and experience gained over the years. This new project became a form of therapy, a way to reconnect with her younger self, the girl who dreamt of weaving stories that touched hearts.

The launch of Rahul's film became a momentous occasion. Celebrities graced the red carpet, cameras flashed, and the air crackled with anticipation. Hemlata, standing by Rahul's side, her heart brimming with pride, watched as their story unfolded on the silver screen. As the credits rolled, the auditorium erupted in applause, a thunderous confirmation of the film's emotional impact.

In the weeks that followed, the film garnered rave reviews, lauded for its nuanced portrayal of love and defiance against societal norms. The experience catapulted Rahul and Hemlata into the spotlight, their names synonymous with courage, passion, and a love story that defied tradition.

However, amidst the fame, Hemlata remained grounded. She continued promoting her novel, the powerful story resonating with readers across generations. It resonated with mothers who understood the quiet sacrifices they made, and with daughters who yearned for a deeper connection with their mothers.

One afternoon, while attending a book signing event, a woman approached Hemlata, tears glistening in her eyes. "Thank you," she said, her voice trembling with emotion. "Your book helped me understand my mother better. It allowed me to see her sacrifices and forgive myself for the years of misunderstanding."

Hemlata felt a surge of gratitude. Her story, born from personal loss and reconciliation, had the power to heal others, to bridge the gap between generations, and to foster empathy and understanding.

As Hemlata returned to her writing desk, the city lights twinkling outside her window, she knew this was just the beginning of a new chapter. She wasn't just a writer who defied tradition; she was a voice for the voiceless, a storyteller who wove tales of love, loss, and the enduring human spirit.

And with every word she wrote, she carried the legacy of her mother's love, the courage she instilled, and the unwavering belief in the power of stories to heal and inspire.

Years flowed by, etching themselves onto the canvas of Hemlata and Rahul's life. Their cozy apartment, a haven for creativity, had expanded to accommodate a small study for Hemlata and a dedicated workspace for Rahul, now an established screenwriter. The bookshelves overflowed not just with their own acclaimed works but also with the stories of aspiring writers they mentored.

Hemlata's name was no longer just on book covers; it graced university syllabuses as a testament to her literary prowess. Her novel about mothers and daughters, a poignant exploration of love and sacrifice, became a bestseller, translated into multiple languages and earning her a coveted literary award.

Their lives, however, weren't confined to the four walls of their apartment or the bright lights of book launches and film premieres. They continued to host workshops, offering guidance and encouragement to budding writers.

Hemlata's workshops, filled with warmth and insightful discussions, became known for their nurturing environment.

One day, amidst the clutter of manuscripts and aspiring writers' notes, a familiar face caught Hemlata's eye. It was Priya, her childhood friend, now a published author herself. Their reunion was filled with laughter, shared memories, and a sense of pride in each other's achievements.

Hemlata and Priya reminisced about their childhood dreams, the stolen moments spent reading under the banyan tree, and Hemlata's defiant escape to the city. Priya confessed that Hemlata's courage had inspired her to pursue her own writing career, despite societal pressures to choose a more "practical" path.

As their conversation flowed, an idea sparked in Hemlata's mind. "Priya," she exclaimed, her eyes gleaming with excitement, "remember the stories we used to write together? Why don't we collaborate on a book – a collection of tales woven from our childhood experiences?"

Priya's face lit up with a smile. "It would be a wonderful tribute to our friendship," she agreed.

The prospect of collaborating with her childhood friend, the friend who had supported her secret meetings with Rahul, filled Hemlata with a sense of joy. It was a way to revisit their roots, to celebrate their shared journey, and to showcase the power of female friendships that blossomed even amidst societal expectations.

News of their collaboration spread quickly, generating excitement among their readers. The book, a charming blend of nostalgia and introspection, became an instant success. It resonated with readers who craved stories about the enduring power of childhood friendships and the unwavering support found in true companions.

As Hemlata and Priya basked in the success of their collaboration, they realized their journey had come full circle. They had defied expectations, followed their passions, and emerged as successful writers, their voices now reaching a global audience.

One evening, as they sat on their balcony overlooking the city lights, Rahul turned to Hemlata, a question lingering in his eyes. "Have you given any thought to revisiting your childhood stories?" He inquired, gesturing towards a stack of dusty manuscripts on a nearby table.

Hemlata smiled, a warm wave of nostalgia washing over her. The stories, filled with a child's wonder and unbridled imagination, suddenly held a new appeal. "Perhaps," she replied, "it's time to dust them off and let them find their voice."

The city lights twinkled below, reflecting in Hemlata's eyes as she envisioned her next project. It wouldn't be a story of defiance or overcoming societal norms. It would be a return to her roots, a celebration of the spark that ignited her love for storytelling, a story woven with the magic of childhood dreams and the enduring power of imagination.

Chapter 5: Whispers of Imagination

The rhythmic clatter of the keyboard had become the soundtrack of Hemlata's life. Hunched over her desk, bathed in the warm glow of her study lamp, she wrestled with the complexities of her new project. It wasn't the usual heart-wrenching social commentary or the poignant exploration of human relationships that had become her trademark. This was a journey back in time, a dive into the fantastical world she had created as a child.

Dusting off the forgotten manuscripts, Hemlata rediscovered a treasure trove of stories – tales of talking animals, enchanted forests, and brave princesses on mythical quests. Each page whispered with the innocence and boundless imagination of a child yearning to escape the confines of reality.

As she reread her childhood stories, Hemlata felt a sense of wonderment wash over her. The simple, yet whimsical plots, were imbued with a raw honesty that resonated with her even now. In these fantastical worlds, she had found a voice, a way to express the anxieties and dreams that swirled within her young mind.

However, revisiting these stories also presented a challenge. They were written in a naive voice, devoid of the technical mastery she possessed as a mature author. Hemlata wrestled with the question – how to bridge the gap between the raw emotion of her childhood stories and the refined storytelling skills she had honed over the years?

Days turned into weeks as Hemlata meticulously reviewed her childhood creations. She meticulously analyzed the plotlines, the character arcs, and the underlying themes that resonated even now. Slowly, a plan began to take shape.

She wouldn't rewrite them entirely; instead, she would act as a curator, preserving the essence of her childhood imagination while weaving in the technical expertise she had gained.

The process became a journey of self-discovery. As Hemlata breathed life into these old stories, she reconnected with the little girl who yearned to escape into fantastical worlds. She remembered the solace found in creating stories, the sheer joy of weaving narratives that transported her beyond the boundaries of her everyday life.

One afternoon, while sharing her work with Rahul, she confessed her initial apprehension.

"What if these stories seem childish? What if they don't resonate with my readers after all?"

Rahul, ever her source of comfort and encouragement, took her hand in his. "Hemlata," he said, his voice filled with warmth, "these stories hold a unique charm. They're unfiltered, raw, and speak directly to the child within us all. Don't underestimate the power of imagination."

His words resonated with Hemlata. She realized that the very qualities she found "childish" were the very essence of these stories. They were a testament to the pure, unadulterated joy of storytelling, a reminder that the most captivating narratives often stemmed from the simplest of ideas.

Fueled by renewed confidence, Hemlata delved deeper into her project. Late nights were spent rewriting, revising, and polishing her childhood stories. She breathed life into the characters, giving them depth and dimension, while ensuring they retained the innocent charm that made them so endearing.

One of the stories, titled "The Talking Mango Tree," resonated deeply with Hemlata. It was a tale about a young girl who confides in a magical talking tree, seeking solace from the loneliness she felt in her traditional household. As she revisited the story, Hemlata realized it mirrored her own childhood experiences, her yearning for connection and a space to express herself freely.

By weaving in subtle threads of her own experiences, Hemlata transformed the story into a poignant narrative about the importance of communication and the solace found in unlikely friendships. She realized that the power of these stories lay not just in their fantastical elements but also in the subtle reflections of real-life emotions and experiences.

The process of revisiting her childhood stories wasn't just about creating a new book; it was a therapeutic journey. It allowed Hemlata to connect with her younger self, understand her anxieties and dreams, and celebrate the spark that had ignited her lifelong love of storytelling.

Months flew by in a flurry of creative activity. Hemlata's study became a haven for her childhood stories. Sketches adorned the walls, depicting fantastical landscapes and the quirky characters she was bringing to life. Stacks of revised manuscripts filled the shelves, each page a testament to her meticulous revisions.

As Hemlata delved deeper into this project, she began to understand the appeal of children's literature. It wasn't just about simplistic plots and colorful illustrations; it was about creating a world where magic and reality danced hand in hand, where lessons were learned through fantastical adventures, and where imagination held the key to unlocking endless possibilities.

Hemlata found herself captivated by the sheer honesty of her childhood voice. Unafraid of exploring complex emotions like loneliness, frustration, and the yearning for acceptance, the stories resonated with the universality of childhood experiences. She realized that these emotions, though presented through talking animals and enchanted forests, were relatable to children of all ages and backgrounds.

One evening, Rahul arrived home from a meeting, a weariness etched on his face. As he settled on the sofa, Hemlata handed him a freshly printed manuscript titled "The Whispering

WOODS: A COLLECTION of Tales."

"This is your childhood stories, isn't it?" Rahul asked, a hint of curiosity in his voice.

Hemlata nodded, her eyes filled with a nervous anticipation. "I've been working on revising them."

Rahul spent the next few hours engrossed in the stories. A smile played on his lips as he encountered familiar characters and fantastical settings. He chuckled at the antics of the mischievous talking squirrel and felt a pang of empathy for the lonely princess yearning for a true friend.

When he finished the last story, he looked at Hemlata, his eyes sparkling with excitement.

"Hemlata," he exclaimed, "these stories are magical! They're whimsical, heartwarming, and packed with hidden lessons."

His genuine enthusiasm warmed Hemlata's heart. "But what about the writing style? Don't you think it's too simplistic for my usual readers?"

Rahul shook his head. "Not at all. The simplicity is what makes them so charming. It allows the imagination to take flight. Besides, beneath that simplicity lies a depth of emotion that will resonate with children and adults alike."

His words instilled in Hemlata a renewed confidence. She realized that the very qualities she had initially questioned – the simplicity of the language and the unadulterated expression of emotions – were the very strengths of these stories.

FINDING THE PERFECT Voice

The next step was finding the right illustrator. Hemlata knew that the success of her book hinged on captivating visuals that complemented the fantastical elements of her stories. Through her network of writer friends, she connected with a young illustrator named Maya, whose whimsical sketches and vibrant colors perfectly captured the essence of her childhood imagination.

Maya, upon reading Hemlata's stories, was instantly captivated. Her sketches brought the characters and settings to life with a flourish, capturing the playful spirit of the talking animals and the awe-inspiring beauty of the enchanted forests. As Hemlata reviewed Maya's illustrations, she felt a sense of satisfaction wash over her. The stories were no longer just words on paper; they were transforming into a vibrant, interactive world ready to be unveiled to the world.

FACING THE CRITICS

The release of "The Whispering Woods: A Collection of Tales" was met with a mix of anticipation and curiosity. Hemlata's established fans, accustomed to her poignant social commentaries, were intrigued by this foray into children's literature. Critics, too, were eager to see how a renowned author known for her complex characters and nuanced storytelling would navigate the simpler world of children's books.

The reviews poured in, and to Hemlata's delight, they were overwhelmingly positive. Critics lauded the book for its captivating narratives, its charming illustrations, and its ability to transport readers to worlds brimming with imagination.

Parents praised it for its ability to spark children's curiosity, ignite their love for storytelling, and subtly address real-life challenges they might be facing.

One review, penned by a renowned children's literature critic, resonated deeply with Hemlata.

"Hemlata Patel's 'The Whispering Woods' reminds us that the best stories often begin with a child's wonder," the review stated. "These tales, unburdened by the complexities of adult life, tap into the universal longing for adventure, friendship, and a connection with something magical. They are a testament to the power of imagination and a reminder that sometimes, the simplest stories leave the most profound impact."

The success of "The Whispering Woods" opened a new chapter in Hemlata's literary career. She found herself enjoying the connection with younger readers, conducting school visits, and participating in book readings where she witnessed firsthand the joy her stories brought to children'

The success of "The Whispering Woods" brought a sense of joy and fulfillment to Hemlata's life. Beyond the critical acclaim and commercial success, it rekindled a love for storytelling that transcended age and genre. Witnessing the magic her stories weaved in young minds ignited a passion for nurturing future storytellers.

Hemlata and Maya, the illustrator, embarked on a series of school visits. Witnessing children's faces light up as Maya sketched the fantastical creatures from the book and Hemlata narrated the tales in a voice brimming with warmth brought immense satisfaction. The interactive sessions allowed Hemlata to connect with a new generation of readers, planting seeds of creativity and a love for literature.

One afternoon, during a visit to a bustling elementary school library, Hemlata found herself surrounded by a group of wide-eyed children. As she finished reading a story from "The Whispering Woods," a small hand shot up.

"Will you write more stories about the talking animals?" a little girl with pigtails asked, her voice filled with curiosity.

Hemlata smiled. "Perhaps I will," she replied.

"What kind of adventures would you like them to have?"

The children erupted in a cacophony of ideas, each more imaginative than the last. They wanted the talking squirrel to embark on a treasure hunt, the wise old owl to share stories from the past, and the shy princess to find her voice and lead her kingdom.

Hemlata listened intently, her heart brimming with

inspiration. These children, their faces aglow with excitement, ignited a spark within her. She realized that the world of "The Whispering Woods" wasn't just a collection of stories; it was a universe brimming with possibilities, waiting to be explored.

BUILDING A COMMUNITY

Back in her cozy apartment, Hemlata began brainstorming new adventures for the characters in "The Whispering Woods." She found herself drawn back to her childhood, remembering the solace she found in creating stories in dusty notebooks.

This time, however, she wanted to involve her readers. Inspired by the children's suggestions, Hemlata launched an online forum dedicated to "The Whispering Woods." Here, children could share their own stories set in the fantastical world, discuss their favorite characters, and even suggest ideas for future adventures.

The forum became a vibrant space for creativity. Children from across the globe shared their stories, some whimsical and funny, others poignant and thought-provoking. Hemlata interacted with them regularly, offering encouragement and guidance. She found immense joy in fostering a love for storytelling in young minds and witnessing their boundless imagination take flight.

A LEGACY ENDURES

Years passed, and Hemlata's life blossomed in unexpected ways. "The Whispering Woods" series grew into a collection of beloved children's books, translated into multiple languages and cherished by readers of all ages. Hemlata continued writing for adults as well, but her foray into children's literature left a lasting impact.

One fateful day, Hemlata received a letter from a young woman named Sarah. Sarah, now a published author herself, credited Hemlata's stories with igniting her passion for writing. She had participated in the forum as a child, sharing her own fantastical tales and finding encouragement from Hemlata's thoughtful responses.

Reading Sarah's letter filled Hemlata with a sense of profound satisfaction. Her journey, from a defiant young woman yearning to write to a bestselling author and mentor, had come full circle. It wasn't just about her own success; it was about the legacy she was leaving behind – a legacy of stories that sparked imagination, nurtured creativity, and empowered young minds to embrace the magic of storytelling.

As Hemlata sat at her desk, overlooking the bustling city, she knew her journey as a writer wasn't over. New stories, both for adults and children, swirled in her mind. But for now, she basked in the warmth of knowing that her words, born from a childhood filled with dreams and a journey fueled by courage, had touched countless lives and would continue to do so for generations to come.

Hemlata's life resonated with the rhythm of a well-played song. There were crescendos of success, lulls of introspection, and a constant undercurrent of creativity that flowed through everything she did. Writing for adults remained her anchor, allowing her to explore complex themes and social issues. However, her foray into children's literature had opened a new chamber in her heart, one brimming with pure, unadulterated joy of storytelling.

The online forum for "The Whispering Woods" continued to be a thriving space. Children from around the globe contributed stories, poems, and even illustrations, creating a vibrant tapestry of creativity. Hemlata, acting as a benevolent guide, nurtured their talents, offering constructive criticism and celebrating their successes.

Witnessing young minds embrace the magic of words and translate their dreams onto the page filled her with immense satisfaction.

One evening, while browsing the forum, Hemlata stumbled upon a story that sent a shiver down her spine. It was written by a young girl named Priya, a name that resonated from the depths of her memory. As she read the story, a flood of memories washed over her – their childhood pact under the banyan tree, their shared love for storytelling, and the bittersweet parting that followed Hemlata's escape to the city.

Reaching out to Priya through the forum, Hemlata initiated a conversation. They reconnected online, reminiscing about their childhood dreams and the impact it had on their lives. Priya, now a teacher, confessed that Hemlata's defiance had served as a silent inspiration, motivating her to pursue her passion for writing, albeit in a different form.

Their online conversations soon morphed into video calls, filled with laughter, shared memories, and a sense of lost time rediscovered. One day, Priya floated a proposition – a collaboration on a children's book, a story that mirrored their own childhood friendship, filled with dreams, aspirations, and the enduring power of female bonds.

Hemlata's heart soared. This was a story waiting to be told, a tale that celebrated their shared journey, the power of friendship that transcended societal expectations, and the unwavering belief in pursuing one's dreams. The prospect of co-creating a book with her childhood friend, the one who had supported her most daring adventures, filled her with a sense of exhilaration.

News of their collaboration spread like wildfire, igniting excitement among fans and aspiring writers. The book, a heartwarming tale of friendship and defying societal norms, became an instant success. It resonated with young readers, particularly girls, who saw in Hemlata and Priya a reflection of their own struggles and dreams.

The success of their collaboration further cemented Hemlata's legacy as a writer who wasn't afraid to push boundaries. She had defied expectations as a young woman yearning for freedom, as a writer exploring complex themes, and now, as a mentor nurturing future storytellers.

THE SYMPHONY CONTINUES

Years flew by, and Hemlata's life was a tapestry woven with creativity, joy, and a profound sense of fulfillment. The rhythmic clatter of her keyboard continued to be the soundtrack of her days, her stories finding solace in the hearts of readers worldwide.

One crisp autumn afternoon, Hemlata sat on her balcony overlooking the city. Beside her, Rahul held her hand, his eyes twinkling with pride. She glanced towards a bookshelf where a well-worn collection of childhood stories sat, a constant reminder of her journey.

The city lights twinkled below, reflecting in Hemlata's eyes. A faint melody played in the background, a tune that resonated with the rhythm of her life – a life filled with passion, challenges, and the enduring power of storytelling. The symphony wasn't over; it was merely a pause, a moment to reflect before embarking on a new chapter, a new set of stories waiting to be born. For Hemlata, the whispers of imagination would forever guide her, reminding her that the most powerful stories are often rooted in the dreams of a child and the courage to bring them to life.

Conclusion:

Hemlata closed her laptop with a gentle sigh, a satisfied smile gracing her lips. The final chapter of her latest novel lay complete, a testament to her enduring love for storytelling. Glancing out the window, she watched the vibrant city lights flicker on, casting a warm glow over her cozy apartment.

Life, for Hemlata, had become a symphony of stories. From the rebellious teenager yearning to be a writer to the acclaimed author whose words touched hearts across generations, her journey had been a testament to the power of dreams and the courage to defy expectations.

The success of "The Whispering Woods" series continued to bring her immense joy. Children from all corners of the globe wrote to her, their letters filled with tales of how her stories sparked their own creativity. Reading them fueled her passion for nurturing young minds, reminding her that stories had the power to transport them to magical worlds and inspire them to become storytellers themselves.

Her collaboration with Priya remained a highlight of her career. The heartwarming tale of their childhood friendship became a cornerstone of children's literature, reminding young readers of the importance of chasing dreams and the enduring power of female bonds. It cemented Hemlata's legacy as a writer who wasn't afraid to push boundaries, both in her personal life and in her literary pursuits.

One sunny afternoon, a familiar face appeared at her doorstep – Maya, the illustrator who had brought "The Whispering Woods" to life with her vibrant artwork. Maya, now an established children's book illustrator herself, had come to discuss a new project. The idea, a picture book collaboration brimming with whimsical creatures and playful storylines, reignited the spark in Hemlata's eyes.

As Hemlata and Maya brainstormed ideas, a sense of camaraderie filled the room. They were no longer just writer and illustrator; they were partners in creating worlds of wonder for young readers. Hemlata realized that the legacy of her stories wasn't just confined to the pages she wrote; it was woven into the collaborations, the friendships, and the inspiration she shared with others.

Years later, nestled in her armchair surrounded by overflowing bookshelves, Hemlata held a well-worn leather-bound notebook. It contained her childhood stories, the very ones that had sparked her journey. A wave of nostalgia washed over her as she reread the faded ink and remembered the little girl who dreamt of weaving fantastical tales.

Looking back, she realized that the essence of those stories remained unchanged. It was in the simple joy of storytelling, the unfiltered expressions of emotions, and the boundless imagination of a child that her true voice resided.

Hemlata closed the notebook, a tear glistening in her eye. Her journey, filled with defiance, success, and profound connections, had come full circle. The symphony of stories may have reached a crescendo, but like a song with a powerful ending that lingers in the air, the whispers of imagination would forever guide her.

As long as there were dreams to chase and stories to tell, Hemlata knew she would continue to write, her words weaving a legacy that would inspire generations to come.

About the Author

Mrigendra Bharti, born on June 29, 2004, in South Delhi, India, is a multifaceted individual recognized as the owner of Mrigendra Bharti Group InfoTech India Co. Pvt Ltd. Beyond his entrepreneurial endeavors, he is a distinguished music producer, director, and a budding writer.

Embarking on his professional journey at a young age, Mrigendra Bharti's visionary leadership has led to the establishment of several successful ventures, including Croma Music Series Entertainment, Sellbrochure, Fauget Innovative, and more.

What sets Mrigendra apart is his early initiation into the world of business. His foray into the unknown realms of entrepreneurship began during his 10th-grade years, where he delved into the music industry. This initial venture laid the foundation for subsequent achievements, showcasing his dedication and resilience.

Having honed his skills in music, Mrigendra Bharti not only demonstrated significant growth in his craft but also expanded his professional network. His passion extends beyond music, encompassing app and website development, as well as graphic design.

Fueled by his creative aspirations, Mrigendra established the Mrigendra Bharti Group, a company specializing in website and app development. Currently, he collaborates with a dedicated team, collectively working on ambitious projects that promise innovation and excellence.

Mrigendra's journey serves as an inspiration, particularly for today's students, highlighting the potential of youthful determination and the ability to transform innovative ideas into successful businesses. As he continues to make strides in various domains, Mrigendra Bharti remains a dynamic force, contributing vibrancy to the realms of business, music, and technology.

Read more at https://www.imwriter-mrigendra.rf.gd.